ZOO

With thanks to Joseph for his
invaluable contribution.
A.B.

ZOO

A Red Fox Book

ISBN 978 0 09 921901 9

First published by Julia MacRae Books 1992
Red Fox edition published 1994
an imprint of Random House Children's Publishers UK
A RANDOM HOUSE GROUP COMPANY

27 29 30 28

Addresses for companies within The Random House Group Limited
can be found at: www.randomhouse.co.uk/offices.htm

www.randomhousechildrens.co.uk

Printed in China

ZOO

ANTHONY BROWNE

Red Fox

My Family

Me.

My brother.

Dad.

Mum.

Last Sunday we all went to the zoo.
Me and my brother were really excited.

But there were masses of cars on the road, and it took ages to get there. After a while Harry and I got really bored. So we had a fight. Harry started crying and Dad told me off. It's not fair, he never tells Harry off, it's always *my* fault.

"What kind of jam do you get stuck in?" asked Dad.

"Don't know," said Harry.

"A traffic jam!" roared Dad.

Everyone laughed except Mum and Harry and me.

When we finally got there Dad *had* to
have a row with the man in the ticket
booth. He tried to say that Harry was only
four, and should get in half-price. (He's
five-and-a-half actually.)

"Daylight robbery!" Dad snarled.
Sometimes he can be really embarrassing.

We hadn't got a map of the zoo so we just wandered round. Me and my brother wanted to see the gorillas and monkeys, but we had to see all these boring animals first. We went into the elephant house which was really smelly. The elephant just stood in a corner stuffing its face.

Mum had brought some chocolate and
Harry and I were starving. "Can we have
it now?" I asked.

    "No, not yet," said Dad.

    "Why not?" whined Harry.

    "Because," said Dad.

    "Because what?" I asked.

    "Because I say so," said Dad.

It seemed he was in one of his moods.

Then we saw the tigers. One of them was just walking along a wall of the cage, then turning round and walking all of the way back. Then it would start again.

"Poor thing," said Mum.

"You wouldn't say that if it was chasing after you," snorted Dad. "Look at those nasty teeth!"

Harry and I were getting really hungry.
"Can't we have lunch now?" I asked.
"But we've only just got here," said Mum.
It seemed like we'd been there for hours.
My brother thumped me, so I kicked him
and we wrestled for a bit, then Dad told
me off.

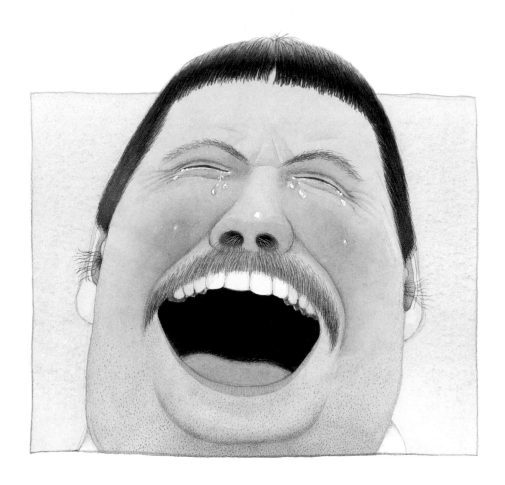

We looked at the penguins next. I usually
find penguins funny when I see them on
the telly, but all I could think of was food.

"What animal can you eat at the zoo?"
asked Dad.

"Don't know," I groaned.

"A hot dog!" howled Dad. He was holding
his stomach and laughing so much that
tears were rolling down his face.

"Come on, boys," said Mum, "let's get
something to eat."

The café was great. I had burger and chips and
beans and loads of tomato ketchup, and a chocolate
ice-cream with raspberry sauce. It was brilliant.

After that we went into the gift shop to spend
our pocket money. We each bought a funny monkey hat.
"Which one is the monkey?" jeered you-know-who.
Then we had to go and see the polar bear. It looked
really stupid, just walking up and down, up and down.

Next we saw the baboons, and they were a bit more interesting. Two of them had a fight. "They remind me of someone," said Mum. "I can't think who."

The orang-utan crouched in a corner and didn't move. We tried shouting at it and banging on the glass, but it just ignored us. Miserable thing.

Finally we found the gorillas, they were quite good. Of course Dad had to do his King Kong impersonation, but luckily we were the only ones there.

Then it was time to go home. In the car Mum asked us what was the best bit of the day. I said the burger and chips and beans, and Harry said the monkey hats.

Dad said the best bit was going home, and asked her what was for dinner.

"I don't think the zoo really is for animals," said Mum. "I think it's for people."

That night I had a very strange dream.

Do you think animals have dreams?

Other books by Anthony Browne

My Dad

My Mum

My Brother

The Night Shimmy

The Shape Game

Voices in the Park

Willy and Hugh

Willy the Wizard